dedicated
to the special ME
in all of us

Love
is a flower
that grows
in the sun,

and a playful
kitten who wants
to have fun.

Love
is a warm place
when winter
is cold,

and a
caring grandma
to snuggle
and hold.

Love
is a teacher
who makes
us feel good

when we've
done our work
the best that
we could.

Love
is a friend
who gives
us a hug

when we're
feeling sad
and our heart
strings go tug.

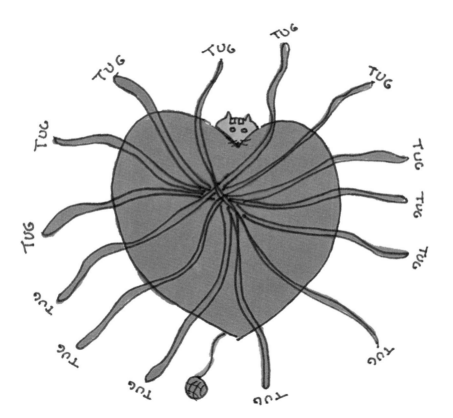

Love
is a rainbow,
a kiss in
the sky

when sunshine
and raindrops
together go by.

are gifts
of love that
we feel in
our hearts,

that come
from inside us
where all of
love starts.

So ...
stretch out
your arms

and wrap
them 'round
tight,

loving yourself
with all of
your might.